The Magic Hare

Collins
RED
STORYBOOK

The Magic Hare

Twelve Tales by
Lynne Reid Banks
Illustrated by Hilda Offen

Collins
An imprint of HarperCollinsPublishers

First published in Great Britain by HarperCollins in 1992
First published in paperback in Young Lions in 1993
This edition published in Collins in 1998
Collins is an imprint of HarperCollins*Publishers* Ltd
77-85 Fulham Palace Road, Hammersmith, London, W6 8JB

1 3 5 7 9 8 6 4 2

Text copyright © Lynne Reid Banks 1992
Illustrations copyright © Hilda Offen 1992

ISBN 0 00 765352 2

The author and illustrator assert the moral right to
be identified as the author and illustrator of the work.

Printed and bound in Great Britain by
Bookmarque Ltd, Croydon, Surrey

Contents

To Theatre of the Heart
where Hare began.

The Hare and the Spoilt Queen

O nce there was a spoilt queen. She was bad tempered and terribly unfair. She blamed her people for everything that went wrong.

For instance, at her coronation, just as the Archbishop set the crown on her head, she bent over to scratch a sudden itch on her instep and her crown fell off and rolled down the steps leading to the throne.

She ranted and raved that it was everyone's fault but hers, and spoilt the whole occasion so thoroughly that nobody took pictures of her. Then she got furious again because her picture wasn't in the papers or on television. She closed all the TV stations and newspapers down, so nobody knew what was happening.

To cheer her up, her people held a big

festival for her. They planned it weeks in advance and worked very hard to make it a success. When the day came – it rained. The queen jumped up and down, shouting that it was all their fault for choosing a rainy day to hold the festival on.

All the people felt very miserable. The queen wasn't speaking to anyone. There was no telly. Nobody knew what to do.

One day the spoilt queen was out walking in the palace garden with two scared ladies-in-waiting. They kept just behind her and held hands because they were so frightened that she would find something to blame them for.

She pulled an apple crossly off a tree and bit into it. Then she spat out the piece, turned on the two ladies-in-waiting and screamed:

"This apple is *sour*! How dare you let me pick it when it's not ripe!"

And she threw it straight at them.

They didn't bother arguing that it wasn't their fault. They just turned and ran.

That left the queen on her own. She stamped and fumed in the long grass, shouting at the top of her voice: "I HATE EVERYONE!" But suddenly, just near her stamping feet, she saw a little furry head with long ears.

She stopped carrying on, and said: "Oh! A hare in my orchard!" She didn't know whether to be pleased or annoyed, but as usual she chose to be annoyed. "You're trespassing, hare! Go away at once."

"Oh, all right," said the hare. "If you prefer to be alone." And he hopped off.

"Wait!" cried the queen imperiously. The hare stopped and looked back. "I didn't know you could talk. That makes a difference. Come back and talk to me." She was used to ordering everyone about, but the hare didn't move.

"Come here, I said!" shouted the spoilt queen, stamping her foot.

"'Please' would be nice," said the hare.

"'PLEASE'!" echoed the queen. "A queen doesn't have to say 'please'!" The mere idea shocked her.

"Well, I don't know much about queens, but personally I don't like talking to *anyone* who doesn't say please. *And* thank you," said the hare very reasonably.

"You impertinent little animal!" cried the queen. "Do you presume to teach me manners?"

"Not at all," said the hare. "I don't care how you behave. All I said was that 'please' would be nice. Because I like things nice." And he made off in great bounds, ignoring the queen's shouts at him to come back immediately.

That night the queen summoned her gamekeeper.

"There's a hare in the orchard," she said. "I want him for the pot. Shoot him."

The gamekeeper trembled in his boots.

"That hare can't be shot, Your Majesty," he muttered. "He's a magic hare. If you try to shoot him, he vanishes."

"A magic hare! I should have guessed," said the queen. "Then trap him for me – I want him alive."

"He can't be trapped either, Ma'am."

"Then how am I to get my hands on him? I want him for my very own magic hare!"

The gamekeeper shook his head. "Nothing to be done," he said.

"This is all your fault, you stupid man!" railed the queen. "It's your job to catch game for me! You're dismissed!"

The gamekeeper, who had five children

to feed, went away sadly. There was a lot of unemployment among gamekeepers.

No sooner was he out of the door than the hare appeared in front of the throne. The queen was so surprised that she jumped.

"How can you be so mean?" he asked indignantly.

"I do as I like! I'm the queen!" screamed the queen.

"More's the pity, if you ask me," muttered the hare.

"What's that you said?"

"I said, more's the pity. I should think your subjects would rather have almost any other queen than you."

The queen's mouth fell open. She was speechless. She had never in her whole life been spoken to like that, not even by her nanny when she was little.

The hare didn't take advantage of her speechlessness to tell her off some more. Instead he did a little dance.

This had an extraordinary effect on the queen. It calmed her down. She sat watching the hare leaping about and her heartbeat slowed, her eyes lost their anger, and her fists unclenched.

Then something very strange happened. She found she had got to her feet and begun dancing, too, jumping and kicking her legs about just like the hare. Fortunately there was no one watching or they would have thought it very undignified.

The hare finished his dance. The queen stopped too, breathless.

"I'm quite thirsty after that!" said the hare cheerfully. "Could you fancy a glass of water?"

"Water? I don't drink—" began the queen faintly. But before she could go on to say she never drank anything less than champagne, she found a glass of water in her hand, and, feeling suddenly very thirsty, she drank some.

It was perfectly delicious! The most satisfying, cooling, thirst-quenching drink she'd ever drunk.

"This is divine!" she cried, and drank the lot. "Lovely and fizzy! Can you make this drink whenever you like?"

"Yes, but so can you. It comes from the spring in your garden."

"I'll never drink anything else!" said the queen. "I feel so good! What can I do to express what I feel?"

"You know," said the hare, and vanished.

The queen sat down and gave the matter some thought.

Then she rang the bell and summoned her chancellor.

"Good morning, my dear Chancellor!" she said.

The poor man nearly fainted.

"I have some instructions for you, *please*, if you would be so very kind. First, call back my gamekeeper and ask him if he would stay in my employ – at double the wages, of course. Next, I am going to open my palace grounds for one day every month and give an enormous fête. Everyone's invited."

"Everyone, Ma'am? You mean, *ordinary* people?"

"They're not ordinary people, they're my people. No expense to be spared. Especially for music. I want the best musicians, who specialise in music to dance to."

"Your commands shall be obeyed, Your Majesty," said the astounded chancellor, bowing low.

"Not commands," said the queen. "Requests. Thank you, Chancellor, that will be all."

The chancellor backed out of the room in the approved manner, but he was in such a state that he tripped and fell over backwards.

The queen helped him up.

"I'm so very, humbly sorry, Your Majesty—" began the chancellor, all of a tremble.

"Entirely my fault," said the queen.

The Hare and the Flower

One night the magic hare was dancing and jumping about more energetically even than usual. The moon was full, and that was when he danced his best, so he was hurling himself about, trying to resist the temptation to use a bit of magic to enable him to jump that little bit higher than he could by himself. He managed not to, and did a really spectacular leap just the same, which carried him four or five feet above the grass that was whispering in the night wind.

He landed again, panting, and shouted:

"That's the finest jump I've ever jumped, and I didn't use magic a bit! What a rotten shame nobody was here to see me" – and suddenly he heard a tinkling sound.

It was like bells – very small, silvery ones.

19

He looked this way and that. He jumped a few ordinary jumps to get his head clear of the top of the grass, to see what had made that sound. But he couldn't see anything.

There are lots of little noises in nature that only small animals would hear or notice. The hare's world, down near the ground, was full of them. But he'd never heard one just like that tinkling bell-sound.

The fact was, in the hare's ears, the ringing had sounded like *applause*. Applause for his Big Jump.

Well, it was a mystery – that was all. Life was full of them. The hare, who didn't like not knowing things, tried to forget about it.

Next night, the hare was strolling down a lane when he saw a bright light. It was a car's headlight that had been left on by mistake. A number of moths were battering themselves against the hot glass.

"Stop that," said the hare. "You'll bruise yourselves."

"We can't stop!" they cried in frantic little voices. "We have to reach it! We have to!"

He couldn't persuade them, so he worked a small spell on the light, switching it off. The moths breathed sighs of relief and flittered away safely, forgetting to thank him. The hare, feeling a bit miffed, was about to hop off when –

There it was again! That tinkling sound, a little fainter than last night, but quite definite – like somebody, or something, saying "Well done!"

This time the hare was determined to find it. He searched through the grass along the verge, he jumped, he bounced, he called out:

"Who made that tinkling noise? Come on, out with it! Who are you?"

There was no reply.

The hare went to bed in a very puzzled mood.

The next day there was more work to be done.

Down by the river that ran past the hare's home field, he heard the sound of crying, and rushed down to find a poor little cat with its leg torn open by a ferret.

Well, I say "poor little cat" – of course the cat wasn't entirely the innocent victim, it had probably been trying to kill the ferret, but nevertheless it was a poor thing now because its leg was bleeding and it couldn't drag itself along.

The hare had to do some magic very fast to help it home or it would have died there. The hare really could not bear animals dying, and did his best to save them whenever he could. He'd have saved the ferret, too, if it had been getting the worst of it with the cat.

After the cat was safely back in its own garden, with its owner making a big fuss of getting it to the vet, the hare (who was always a bit tired after a big output of magic) lay down in the sun. He had just stretched his back legs out behind and his front legs in front, when he heard that tinkling sound again.

This time he was on a clear bit of ground and it was broad daylight, so he could see much better. He snapped his head towards the sound, and suddenly he saw what was making it.

A pathetic little colourless flower was shaking its bells.

The hare hopped up to it.

"Hallo, Flower," he said.

The flower had never been spoken to

before. Its bells stopped ringing and it seemed to shrink down towards the ground.

"What's your Latin name?" asked the hare politely and importantly. He *loved* the long names of plants and showed off with them.

"Haven't got one," whispered the flower.

"Your common-or-garden name, then," said the hare kindly.

The flower shook its bells sadly.

"*No name at all*?" said the hare, shocked. "But that's terrible! Everything has a name!"

"Not me," whispered the flower. "Nobody's ever bothered. I'm not in any of the garden centres or catalogues. No one ever picks me. I suppose I'm a nothing-flower."

"No you jolly well are not!" exclaimed the hare robustly. "Your bells make the prettiest sound I've ever heard! Tell me," he went on, trying to sound casual, "why were you ringing them just now – and the other night? Were they for me?"

"You did such lovely jumps," whispered the flower. "And you helped those silly moths. And then, just now . . . "

"Yes?" pressed the hare, who loved to hear himself praised.

"You helped that little cat. You're always

helping," it went on in its shy, whispering voice.

"I do my best, of course," said the hare, scratching his ear. "I didn't think anyone had noticed, particularly."

"I did," murmured the flower.

"Well, that's very nice," said the hare. "I mean, one likes to be appreciated."

"What's that?" asked the flower.

"You know – when people notice what you do and give you a word of praise occasionally."

The flower was silent. The hare realised, with a jolt, that it had never been appreciated, ever.

He felt terribly sad suddenly. To go through life never being appreciated – and without even a common-or-garden name!

"Listen," said the hare suddenly. "I'm going to give you a name."

The flower seemed to straighten its stem, and its bells perked up and stood out instead of hanging limply.

"Are you?" it said in a louder whisper than before.

"Yes!" said the hare decisively. "I'm going to name you after me. You are a *harebell*."

At this the flower grew much taller. It stood up above many of the grasses now, and – the hare blinked, was he imagining it? – its flowers took on a brighter colour. They were definitely blue now.

"Fantastic!" it exclaimed, and then added: "I suppose I couldn't have a Latin name too, like other plants?"

That stumped the hare for a second, but he was full of invention and never could admit he couldn't do something.

"Of course you could!" he said. "Your Latin name is – er – *Campanula Rotundifolia.*" He thought that sounded pretty good, and repeated it with a flourish: "Yes. *Campanula Rotundifolia.*"

"Wow," said the Harebell in a voice shaking with awe. "Is that really me?"

"That's you," said the hare firmly.

"What does it mean?"

"'Campanula' means bells. 'Rotund' means round. 'Folia' means leaves. So it means a bell flower with round leaves."

The Harebell shook its bells, which rang out a peal like happy laughter, and turned pink, then white, then blue again.

"See you around then!" said the hare.

"You bet!" shouted the Harebell.

The Hare and the Orphan

There was once a beautiful girl who had been left an orphan when she was very young. Her home was in a little house in a deep, dark forest. Since her parents died, she had never left the clearing around her house, because she was so afraid of the darkness under the trees, the trees themselves, and whatever might lie beyond.

For food she ate the vegetables that grew in her garden, wild fruit that grew in the clearing, and for meat, she set snares and cooked the animals that got caught in them.

One day she found a fine big hare caught in one of her snares.

"Aha! You will make me an excellent supper!" she said.

To her amazement, the hare in her hands spoke to her.

"I shall be honoured to be eaten by such a beautiful woman," it said, in a very pleasing and polite voice.

She was taken aback. But she only said, "Very well, I shall give you that honour."

And she carried the fine hare back to her kitchen.

He didn't struggle, but lay quietly in her arms, looking up at her in a trustful sort of way that made her feel rather uncomfortable, considering that she had quite made up her mind to eat him.

In the kitchen, she laid him on the table and turned away to get the stove burning. She put a pot of water on the stove, then she picked up a sharp knife and turned to him.

She half expected that he would have run away, in fact a bit of her hoped that he had; but he was sitting up on the table with his little front paws tucked to his breast.

"Have you got the onions?" he asked.

"Onions?" she said. "No. Why?"

"Goodness gracious grips! No hare should be cooked without onions," he said reproachfully.

"Oh, all right then," she said, and went out into her garden and pulled up some onions. She left the back door open on purpose, but when she returned the hare was still sitting on the kitchen table.

She prepared the onions and put them in the pot. Then she picked up the knife again.

"And the carrots?" the hare asked.

"You want carrots, too?" asked the girl.

"Of course! Whoever heard of eating hare without carrots?"

So she went outside again and pulled up some carrots. This time she left the door open very wide. But when she came back, the hare was waiting.

She scraped the carrots and put them in the pot. Then she picked up the knife with a strangely heavy heart, and turned to the hare.

"Where's the bayleaf?" he asked.

"Bayleaf?"

"Don't you know about bayleaves? They give a wonderful flavour, especially to hare."

"You insist upon bayleaf?"

"No, I don't insist. But everyone knows that hare doesn't taste its best without a little bayleaf."

She lowered the knife. "I would get some if I could," she said, "just to please you. But I can't."

"Why not? There's a big bay tree just at the far edge of the forest."

The girl shivered.

"I can't go there. I'm too frightened."

The hare looked into her eyes.

"If you're frightened, don't go," he said. "I'll be cooked without a bayleaf."

"But you won't taste your best," she said. "You deserve the very best cooking."

He shrugged. "I don't want you to be frightened. Cook me and eat me now, and enjoy me as much as you can."

And he laid his head on the table.

She put the knife down.

"I'll go and get the bayleaf," she said.

"You're a brave girl. I'll show you the way," said the hare.

They went into the forest together, the hare running ahead, the girl following. It was very dark under the trees. At first she was almost too terrified to walk. But the hare danced along the path in front of her, and after a little while she found herself dancing, too.

At the far end of the forest she saw the bay tree. She saw the wide road. She saw the town in the valley, and the beautiful mountains beyond, and the sky beyond

that. She saw the world she had never seen.

She stopped by the bay tree and cried:

"Look! How lovely it is! And I got here! And I'm not afraid!"

"Pick a leaf and let's go back for supper," said the hare.

She looked at him.

"We'll have carrot and onion soup," she said.

The hare jumped high into the air and landed in her wide-stretched arms. For a second she held him. Then he vanished. And from that time on, she was never afraid of the wood or the world. And she never ate another bite of meat.

The Hare and the Giants

The giant Aspect brothers, whose names were Dismal Aspect and Horrible Aspect, were the terror of the countryside. Especially Horrible.

Dismal was twenty feet tall, but he never stood up straight. He dripped and drooped and shambled and stooped, but when he raised his face, everybody ran away, because he looked so miserable.

Horrible was not so tall but he was immensely fat. When he sat down, it took ten minutes to walk round him. Somebody tried it once and just had time to shout out "Ten minutes!" before Horrible grabbed him and ate him.

Horrible was so ugly that nobody ran away from him, because when they saw him they turned into stone. This made

Horrible furious, because who likes to eat statues? He managed to keep his weight up by grabbing his share of the people Dismal caught by running after them with his long, long legs, but Horrible always complained that his food was too salty. This was due to the runaways crying at Dismal's miserable face.

One day, Dismal caught a couple of people. He and Horrible were fighting over them when they heard a voice crying: "Help, help! I'm caught in a trap!"

The Aspect brothers stopped fighting, dropped their victims and dived towards the sound, hoping to find a nice fat person. But when they found the trap, it was a very small one with just a little hare caught in it.

"Huh, huh, huh!" chortled Horrible. (Dismal never laughed, of course, he was too miserable for that.) "Look! A silly little hare! Shall I step on it, Dizzy? It's not worth eating," and he raised his mighty boot to crush hare and trap together.

"Hey, wait a minute!" called out the hare as the shadow of the boot came down. "I may be little, but I'm worth my weight in gold to you boys!"

Horrible stopped with his foot in the air. Dismal gave him a push and he fell over with a crash that made the top of a mountain fall off.

"How?" asked Dismal dismally. He never expected anything good to happen.

"Let me out and I'll tell you," said the hare.

Dismal had the thinnest fingers, so after a lot of fiddling he managed to open the trap and the hare sprang out.

"Follow me, both of you!" he cried, and set off in great leaps down the hillside. "I'll show you a meal you can't refuse!"

The brothers looked at each other.

"What can he do for us?" gloomed Dismal. "Let's eat those people I—" He looked behind him, but of course they'd run away.

"Come on!" shouted Horrible, who was always hungry, and he went jumping and thundering after the hare. Dismal gave a groan and followed unwillingly.

After running for miles (Horrible just lay down and rolled in the end, it was all downhill) the hare stopped on the edge of a cliff.

"They're down there!" he panted.

"What are?" asked both brothers at once.

"All the people you could ever want," said the hare. "You can eat until you burst, down there!"

Both brothers came to the edge of the cliff and peered over. Down below was a lovely beach with thousands of holiday-makers enjoying themselves on the sand and in the sea. There were bright sunshades and coloured towels and sandcastles with flags on them and people in pretty bathing suits eating picnics and playing games and having a marvellous time.

Horrible looked at Dismal. He was astounded to see that a slow grin was spreading over those dismal features.

"Doesn't it look fun down there!" Dismal said wistfully.

"Never mind 'fun'!" said Horrible. "Doesn't it look like a good dinner! Come on, Diz, let's get to it!"

"How?" said Dismal, who had become dismal again.

"Yes, how?" asked Horrible of the hare. "How do we get down?"

"Jump, of course!" answered the hare.

"JUMP!" exclaimed the brothers. "It's far too far to JUMP!"

But the hare simply said, "Nonsense! Call yourselves giants? Watch me!" And he flung himself off the cliff.

Horrible lost no time. He was starving. He flung himself off the cliff, too. Dismal watched his big fat brother getting smaller and smaller. He saw him land *squash* on eighteen sandcastles. Everyone on the beach rose into the air from the impact. Only Horrible didn't rise into the air.

"Are you all right, Horry?" bawled Dismal.

Horrible didn't answer. Dismal didn't fancy being left out of the feast, but just as he was about to step off the cliff with one long leg, he paused. (He was as stupid as all giants are, but he was a bit cleverer than his brother.)

Where was the hare?

It had entirely disappeared.

Dismal peered downward, trying to make it out among all the people on the beach, who were all now running towards the huge, round hill that was Horrible, and which from their point of view had just dropped from the skies. Dismal could see no sign of any hare. He could see no sign of Horrible jumping up to eat all those people, either.

"Hey, Horry!" roared Dismal, cupping his mouth in his hands.

Not a wiggle out of him that Dismal could see. Just a big fat mountain of flesh. Children were beginning to climb up it. Dismal could see that one rather nimble little boy was already standing on his brother's big, fat, red nose.

"I'm the king of the castle!" the little boy called out.

When he said those words, something extraordinary happened.

Dismal burst out laughing.

It seemed so funny to him, that little boy standing on Horrible's horrible nose and shouting "I'm the king of the castle".

Dismal laughed with all the laughter he'd never used in all his miserable life. He roared with laughter so loud that the people down below looked up at the sky, thinking there was going to be a thunderstorm.

"What's so funny?" asked a small voice beside Dismal.

Dismal, still chortling, looked down. The hare was standing near his left foot.

"It's that little boy. He likes being up there on Horry's nose! He's having a whale of a time climbing on my fat horrible old brother!"

"You were ready to eat that little boy," the hare remarked. "And all the others too."

Dismal stopped laughing and thought about it.

"Yeah, that's true . . . Funny, that . . . Don't fancy them now," he muttered. "Somehow."

"What do you fancy? Fancy a giant pint of beer and a cheese and pickle sandwich and some pork scratchings?"

That same slow, unaccustomed grin spread over Dismal's features.

"D'you know, Hare, that would just hit the spot, that would, now you mention it!"

"Come on, then, let's head for the pub."

The hare set off in great bounds across the hills, with Dismal gallumphing after him. If a giant can skip, he was skipping. By the time they reached the nearest pub, he was whistling.

"That's a jolly tune," said the Hare, "What is it?"

"'Who's Afraid of the Big Bad Giant'," said Dismal, and gave a bellow of laughter. "No one will be, from now on! What're you having, Hare? My shout!"

Quite soon after that, he changed his name. To Cheerful Aspect.

The Hare and the Vampire

When a hare decides to go on holiday, it's usually quite a business. He has to hop to wherever he wants to go, and then just hope he'll find a decent burrow to stay in. By the time he's hopped all the way, say to the seaside, he's so tired he can't enjoy himself much. So most hares just stay at home and make the best of what they're used to.

The magic hare, of course, didn't have to bother with all this. If he wanted to go somewhere, he just wished himself there, and there he was.

The only trouble was, he had to have some definite destination in mind, and he didn't know many places to wish himself to.

One day he was thinking about a holiday,

and not wanting to go to any of the boring old places he'd been before, when suddenly he had an idea.

He crouched in the long grass beside a lane. After a while, a boy came past, and the hare jumped out in front of him.

"Where would you go on holiday if you could go anywhere you liked?" he asked.

"Transylvania," replied the boy at once.

"Trans-where?" asked the hare. "What sort of a place is that?"

"I read about it in a book," said the boy. "It's exciting there. Lots of vampires."

"Really!" said the hare. "How interesting! Well, thanks." And he hopped back into the grass.

He had never heard of vampires and hadn't a clue what they were, but the boy had sounded very enthusiastic. No doubt vampires were something nice like sand-dunes to slide down, or woods to go exploring in, or perhaps delicious things to eat that you couldn't get at home.

Without delay the hare shut his eyes and wished himself in Transylvania.

He opened his eyes and found he was at the top of a mountain, facing a tall and gloomy mansion. It was night, and a full moon shone down on the black turrets and chimneys. Bats flitted about. It was very cold and very quiet. The hare shivered. He didn't think much of Transylvania so far.

"I wonder where the vampires are," he thought.

Just at that moment he saw a strange shape flitting round the turrets and chimneys. It looked like an enormous bat, but it wasn't. It was a man with a big cloak. The hare saw the strange figure climb into the mansion through a skylight.

The hare wished himself inside the mansion. He wanted to see what this funny-looking bat-like man was up to.

Hare found him tiptoeing about in the attic on creaking floorboards. Seen up close, he was decidedly scary. He had shiny hair plastered to his head, eyes that glowed in the dark, and a big, red-lipped mouth.

"Are you looking for something?" asked the hare politely.

The weird man swung round with a snarl, and the hare saw his teeth for the first time. They were the scariest thing of all. They were all jagged and pointy. The hare couldn't help jumping backwards, away from him.

"Who are you? What are you doing here?" growled the man.

"I'm on holiday," said the hare, trying to sound careless.

"On *holiday*? *Here*?" asked the man in astonishment. "Why?"

"This *is* Transylvania, isn't it?"

"Yes."

"Well! I was told it's a very nice place," said the hare. "There are vampires here, you know."

The man stared at him with his glowing eyes, and then suddenly put his head back and let out a bark of laughter.

"You don't say so," he said. "Vampires! And what does a vampire look like, little hare, eh? Would you know one if you met one?"

"Er – well," said the hare, feeling embarrassed. "I imagine they're a . . . well, a feature of the landscape, or . . . possibly some sort of . . . erm. They're a well-known local attraction, anyway."

"A local attraction, are they?" echoed the strange man with an evil chuckle. "I didn't realise that! Well, now you're here, we can't disappoint you, can we? I must show you the sights!"

With that he swooped down on the hare and picked him up by the ears.

"Come with me, my little tourist," he said.

Before the hare knew what was happening, he found himself swiftly carried down a flight of stairs, along a dark corridor and into a huge room. It had a four-poster bed in it with dark curtains, and fast asleep in the bed was a beautiful young girl.

The hare could see her by the light of six candles that burnt in a silver candlestick on the bedside table. The girl's fair hair lay across her pillow; her hands were folded on the edge of the sheet.

The man put the hare on the end of the bed.

"Sh!" he whispered with his finger to his lips. "We mustn't wake her! Not too soon, anyway," and he gave another of his evil chuckles.

The hare, feeling more and more uneasy, watched as the man threw his cloak back over his shoulders. He smiled at the hare, baring those awful teeth, then he bent down as if to kiss the girl.

The hare, without knowing he was going to do it, leapt on to the girl's feet, waking her up.

The first thing she saw on opening her eyes, of course, was the man's face.

She let out a shriek.

"EEEEEK! A vampire!"

"I don't believe this!" cried the hare. "*You're* a vampire! You!"

"Yes indeed," said the man, who was now holding the struggling girl by the shoulders. "I'm what you've come all this way to see."

"What are you doing!" cried the hare, jumping up and down on the girl's stomach in his anxiety. "You look as if you're trying to bite her!"

"Well done," said the man, "you've got it. I'm going to bite her and drink her blood, that's what vampires do – didn't you know?"

"That's revolting!" said the hare, and at last remembered to do a bit of magic.

All the vampire's teeth fell out on the floor, plink, plank, plonk. He let the girl go, and she fell back on the bed in a fearful state.

The vampire was in a state, too. He

clapped his hand to his mouth and tried to say something, but all that came out was:

"Mmm-blp-mmmbl-ffflll-mmm!"

"You're disgusting," said the hare. "Biting girls' necks, goodness gracious grips, I've never heard of such a thing. Well, that's the end of your career as a neck-biter. What's that you said?"

At last he made out the words.

"I'll get falff teeff!"

"They only make nice smooth ones," said the hare. "As a vampire you're finished."

The vampire let out a groan and slunk away with his cloak trailing on the ground.

The hare turned to the girl. "Come on, cheer up, it's all over!" he said, wiping her tears with his long ears.

"I've got a pain!" she sobbed.

"Where? In your neck? Did he get you?"

"No! You did! Jumping on me! I've got a sore tummy!"

"Ah!" The hare quickly magicked it away and, jumping to the floor, did a dance to make her laugh.

"Tell me," he panted at the end, leaping back on the bed again. "is there anything else to do in Transylvania, except rescue girls from vampires?"

"Not a lot," she said with a sigh, stroking him. "It's a boring old place if you ask me."

"So why did that boy say it would be exciting?" wondered the hare.

The Hare and the Lazy Hunter

O nce there was a hunter who was so lazy, he couldn't be bothered to go out to hunt until he was practically starving.

When that happened, he would whistle up his dog.

"Don't just lie about, you lazy beast!" he would say, as the dog shambled to his side. "Get out of here and catch me some game!"

The dog, who was just about as lazy as his master, would heave a deep sigh, and walk very slowly out of the door, pausing on the way to sit down and scratch a flea.

His master would fly into a rage.

"What's the use of you?" he would shout. "Get on with it, and never mind scratching your worthless hide!"

At this the dog would put on a turn of speed and run off into the countryside – run as fast as it could, until it was out of sight of the hunter's cottage. Then it would lie down and doze in the sun, hoping some idiotic creature would run so close to its mouth that he could catch it without any effort.

One day the dog was lying like that, half asleep, when a big, fat hare came jumping along the path.

The dog opened one eye and watched it, rolling its eye up and down as the hare bounded along.

"It doesn't see me!" thought the dog, although he was lying right across the path. "Perhaps it thinks I'm a log and will try to jump over me! Then I can grab its legs without even getting up!"

But when the hare had nearly reached it, it stopped, sat down, and scratched its long ear with one long back foot. Just the way the dog did when it had a flea.

The dog forgot it was supposed to be a log and lifted its head.

"Do hares get fleas, too?" it asked interestedly.

The hare jumped in the air as if it had had a great fright.

"Goodness gracious grips!" it exclaimed. "You're a DOG! I thought you were a bit of wood."

"That's what I meant you to think," said the dog, very pleased with itself.

"You really fooled me," said the hare. "You look exactly like a log."

The dog, which was black and white, was stupid enough to believe every word the hare said.

"If you'd jumped over me," it said, "do you know what I was going to do?"

"No, what?" asked the hare, making big eyes.

"I was going to catch you by the legs and carry you home to my master, who's a hunter."

"Goodness gracious grips!" said the hare again. "How clever! How daring! And you nearly succeeded!"

"Yes! But I didn't quite," said the dog, looking crestfallen. "So now I'll have to go back to my master with nothing, and he'll be angry and beat me."

"BEAT you?" said the hare. "We can't have that! I tell you what. You pick me up in your mouth – very gently, mind – and carry me back to your master. Then he'll be very pleased, and not beat you."

The dog thought this was a brilliant idea. He jumped up, picked up the hare in its mouth – very gently – and carried it back to its master's cottage.

As it came in through the door, the lazy hunter woke from a snooze by the fire, feeling hungrier than ever. He saw the fat hare hanging from the dog's mouth.

"What! A lazy animal like you caught such a big hare! I'd never have believed it!" he exclaimed. "All right, drop it. Leave!"

At this command, the dog let go of the hare, which promptly jumped up and began to leap about the room.

"You stupid hound!" shouted the hunter. "You were meant to kill it! Chase it, you fool, catch it at once!"

The dog chased it, the hunter chased it, they ran all round the cottage five times, but the hare outwitted them at every turn. It made them fall over each other and bump into each other and trip each other up, until the dog was black and blue instead of black and white, and the hunter was purple in the face with rage.

"I'll get it if it's the last thing I ever do!" he vowed.

At last they cornered the hare in an upstairs room.

"Now we've got it!" panted the hunter, who had never run so fast or used so much energy in his life.

The dog and the hunter crept towards the hare, which stood there looking at them without a trace of fear. At the moment when they both made a dive for it, it gave one last great leap in the air. It leapt right up to the ceiling, and they crouched, expecting to feel it land across their backs with its sharp claws.

But they felt nothing.

Fearfully, they both looked up.

The hare had completely disappeared.

The lazy hunter slunk downstairs, exhausted. He didn't have the strength to beat the dog. Instead he opened a tin of baked beans, but before either of them could eat any, they were asleep and snoring.

The Hare
That Cured Hiccups

There was once a prince who was everything a prince ought to be. He was young, tall, handsome and headstrong. He was heir to a large, wealthy kingdom. He knew all the martial arts and he could even play Scrabble.

Every eligible princess in the world had her heart set on him, and they all pestered their kingly fathers without let-up to arrange for them to marry this divine prince.

But none of them knew the prince's Awful Secret. If they had, they would have set all his advantages at naught, even the Scrabble.

The prince suffered from hiccups. Not just ordinary, quickly-got-rid-of hiccups, but *chronic* hiccups. That means that once started, he found it almost impossible to stop hiccing.

He got them when he ate or drank; when he lost at Scrabble; when his bath was too hot, when his dog barked, and when it began to rain.

He always got them before a fight, which put him off so badly that several times he'd had to turn tail and flee, hiccupping all the way. This did not help his reputation, but the princesses still wanted him – they merely thought he was a bit of a coward. They didn't know about the hiccups.

The prince's father and mother – and his doctor, of course – had tried absolutely everything to cure him, like giving him a fright or making him drink a glass of water while standing on his head. The fright gave him double hiccups. The water made him choke and came squirting out of his nose.

The king and queen were in despair. They were so ashamed! They sent all the princesses' kingly fathers away on various excuses, all of which were lies. They just couldn't tell them the real facts. It was too embarrassing.

One day the prince was out riding and hiccupping. The horse was trotting, but the prince was not rising to the trot. He thought a good bouncing might relieve his hiccups, but all it did was give him a sore bottom.

All of a sudden, a hare ran across his path.

His horse got a fright and shied. The prince fell off, after which his bottom was sorer than ever, but he didn't even notice.

The hiccups had stopped!

He got to his feet and caught the horse, feeling how delicious it was not to be hiccuping. He looked all round. There was the hare, sitting up and looking at him from the ditch.

"Could you do that again, do you think?" he asked the hare.

"What, put the wind up the horse? No problem, guv," said the hare.

"Terrific," said the prince. "Tell you what. Hang around near the palace. When I need you, I'll whistle, like this." He whistled piercingly between his teeth. "You come here, beside the road, and I'll ride past. You dash across my path. Okay?"

"You got it, guv," said the hare.

The prince was free of hiccups all that day. It was a blessed relief. He could talk to people, and eat in comfort, and watch TV with the family without them shouting at him to get out of the room because his hiccups were driving them crazy.

But next morning he found a fly in his mug of coffee, and that set him off straight away. Hic! Hic! Hic! It was ghastly.

He ran to the window and blew an ear-splitting whistle. Then he hurried to the stables, saddled his horse and rode at full gallop down the road to the appointed spot.

Sure enough, out dashed the hare, right under the horse's hooves. The horse reared up with a fearful whinny. The prince duly fell off backwards. He nearly broke his coccyx (that's his tailbone) but what did he care about that? The hiccups had gone!

"Thanks a million, hare," he said as he got to his feet with much difficulty due to the pain in his behind.

"Any time, guv," said the hare, "My pleasure." And off he went.

A week later the prince was wrecked. He was swollen and bruised from head

to foot. His left arm was in plaster. His head was bandaged so that only one eye showed. The doctors wanted to put him in hospital, but he insisted he had to go riding once a day, even though he had to be helped on to the horse. (He never had to be helped off. The hare saw to that.)

The prince, despite all his injuries, had never been happier in his life. He had a certain cure for his hiccups. And when you have a cure for a disease, you don't have the disease.

The only trouble now was that none of the princesses wanted to marry him any more because he looked such a mess.

One day the prince was sprawled on the road. He'd cracked a couple of ribs this time, and had knocked himself right out. The hare, who had been getting very curious, hopped up to him and tickled him with his whiskers. He came slowly to consciousness. The hiccups had gone.

"Excuse me," said the hare. "If you don't mind me asking, what's this caper all about?"

The prince roused himself to the extent of lifting his head.

"Every time my horse throws me," he explained, "it stops my hiccups for a whole day."

The hare sat down and scratched his ear.

"Wouldn't you rather stop the hiccups *without* falling off the horse?"

"Well, naturally, but there's no other way." This thought upset the prince so much that, to his horror, he felt the hiccups start up again. He nearly burst into tears.

The hare watched him hiccing for a moment and then turned his back on him.

The prince thought he was going to run away from him the way everybody else did when he had an attack. But instead, the hare rubbed his tail gently against the prince's throat as he lay on the ground.

The hiccups stopped instantly.

The prince was flabbergasted.

"How did you do that?" he asked.

"Nothing to it," said the hare airily. "I'm a magic hare, aren't I?"

"You couldn't magic me back on my horse, or better still, back in my bed, could you?" asked the poor, rib-cracked prince pitifully.

"Just say the word, guv," said the hare. And a second later, the prince was lying in bed with his ribs strapped up and all his bruises going from black to yellow, which meant they were getting better. The hare was lying on the bed beside him with his tail at the ready.

"Hare, you're my best friend," said the prince. "Don't leave me, will you? I'll teach you to play Scrabble."

"You won't have time," said the hare, and nodded towards the door of the prince's room.

It opened, and in burst half a dozen beautiful princesses, all carrying bunches of grapes and bags of nectarines, bouquets of flowers and huge get-well-soon cards.

"You won't be needing me any more, guv," said the hare. "Married men don't get hiccups, that's a scientific fact!"

"But how can I choose?" wailed the prince as he disappeared behind a wave of princesses.

"I hope you never have a worse problem," said the hare.

The Hare
and the Dragon

One night, the hare was disturbed by shrieks and screams. They were enough to turn a hare white, if he hadn't been white already because it was winter.

But that was another odd thing. Just before the commotion started, the hare found himself awake because of being *too hot*.

Clearly things were not as they should be. The hare determined to stay awake and on watch.

For a week of nights, he crouched in the snow near his home, looking around warily. It was bright moonlight and everything was calm and white.

Suddenly on the seventh night, a shadow passed across the moon. A horrific shadow!

For once, the hare was scared out of his

wits. He turned tail, fled down his burrow and lay trembling in the dark.

He heard the screams and shrieks, but he covered his long ears with his paws and pretended not to.

He couldn't sleep for the rest of the night.

The next morning he crept out. Not a hundred yards from home he found a place where the snow had all been melted. Trees had scorched branches. The grass under the snow was burnt right away. And in the mud there were huge footprints.

The footprints of a gigantic dragon!

The hare realised the shrieks had come from some luckless maiden, whom the dragon had swooped down to carry off. The burnt place was from its fiery breath.

The hare couldn't think what to do. He knew that if he confronted the dragon, before he could do any magic tricks the dragon could burn him up. Or gobble him up.

The hare lay in his burrow, trembling and thinking, for a week. It was very tempting to forget the whole thing. But the maiden's shrieks were still echoing in his ears.

He couldn't let that go on! He would have to do something.

At the end of the week, the hare again woke up feeling too hot. This time he raced to the mouth of his hole, which was all aglow from the dragon's flaming breath. He was in time to see a tree burst into flames, and then the huge body of the dragon came to land not fifty yards from where he crouched!

It curved its neck, lashed its tail, and beat its hooked wings, blowing all the trees and bushes about. Its huge eyes glared through the dark as it looked around for prey.

Then it walked, growling and breathing fire, towards the nearest house.

The hare hopped silently over the slushy snow behind it.

When it reached the house, the dragon didn't waste any time. It swung its great tail round and struck off the roof with one blow. Then it stuck its head in through the hole.

A moment later it lifted its head again. A kicking, screaming maiden was in its jaws!

The hare nearly passed out with terror,

but he managed not to. If the dragon wanted to breathe fire now, it would have to drop the maiden. Oddly enough, dragons don't like cooked food.

The hare nerved himself for action.

Scampering round behind the dragon, he leapt on its tail, which had now stopped lashing and was trailing along the ground.

As the dragon prepared to heave its huge body into the air, the hare nimbly ran along the whole length of the tail, up over the spiky back, along the snake-like neck and on to the head between the ears! The dragon's skin, luckily, was so thick it didn't feel a thing.

The worst moment was when the dragon became airborne and the hare looked down to see the ground getting further and further away. Would he ever get back alive? But the maiden was still alive, and kicking. That gave him courage.

Hanging on to a pair of head-scales with his front paws, the hare put his face into one of the dragon's ears and began whispering.

"I'm so good at what I do! I'm such a clever dragon!"

The dragon, as it flew through the night, shook its head a little. But what the strange voice was saying pleased it. (Dragons are not very bright as a rule.)

"Another maiden carried off! And nobody dares to challenge me. I must be the most terrifying dragon in the world!"

This time the dragon nodded, and the hare nearly slipped down his nose, but he managed to hang on by hooking his back feet round the last spike on the dragon's long neck.

"This maiden's family ... They know all about me now! I bet they're crying their eyes out. I bet they hate me."

This was an experiment to see if the dragon had any decent feelings. But it just nodded harder than ever, making the maiden groan as if she might be air-sick.

"Trouble is," whispered the hare, "only a few people know how terrifying I am. I only carry off about one maiden a week ... that's not much when you think of the whole world! Most of the rest probably don't even believe in dragons."

The dragon gave a gusty sigh that almost blew the maiden away, but her nightgown was hooked on one of its teeth.

"Now," went on the hare, "if I could just show the world what a fearful, frightful, horrible, ferocious, terrifying creature I am – so that ABSOLUTELY EVERYONE was afraid of me – that would really be something!"

This time the dragon nodded so violently that it did drop the maiden, and the hare had to pause to give her a magic parachute to help her safely to earth. He managed to magic a little wind to blow her back to her house at the same time. It was the first magic he'd used.

The dragon didn't even notice she'd gone. He was giving snorts and snarls and puffing out gouts of flames that lit up the sky.

The hare took a firmer grip, and whispered in the huge ear:

"I know what! I'll fly all around the world three times, breathing fire, roaring and beating the air with my wings! That'll show them!"

The dragon was so delighted with this idea, which it thought was its own, that it turned four somersaults in the air and nearly set light to its own tail. Then it set off on its endless journey.

Before it got even halfway around the world, it was panting with tiredness. It couldn't breathe even a puff of smoke, and its wings felt as if they were dropping off. But the little voice went on and on:

"I'm not tired! I haven't started yet! There are millions of people who still aren't afraid of me! I've made up my mind, and I'll do it! Three times round, or bust!"

The dragon had just made it back to its starting point, right above the hare's burrow, when it flaked out completely, fizzled this way and that around the sky for a bit like a balloon that's lost its string, and crashed to the ground. There it lay like a green scaly mountain, showing no sign of life.

The hare jumped lightly off its head. He was proud of himself. He had defeated the dragon without using any magic at all, just brains!

He did a little dance in the snow, popped the roof of the maiden's house back on with a wave of his paw, and hopped off to bed.

The Hare and the Black-and-White Witch

S ome shocking news was being whispered about.

A *witch* had moved into the neighbourhood.

All the respectable, decent people were naturally appalled. A witch! Good grief, anything could happen with a witch for a neighbour! Evil goings-on ... Spells ... Honest folk being changed into goodness knows what!

The hare decided to take action.

There was no secret about where the witch was living. She had bought (with what appeared to be ordinary money) a broken-down old house, which seemed entirely suited to be a witch's home. It was grey and dark and damp-looking, it had lots of sticky-out bits – bay windows, turrets and so on – topped off with a spire shaped like a witch's hat.

The hare knew the old house well. It had been empty for years and was practically falling down. So he was very surprised, as he hopped through the big old iron gates, to see that the house looked completely different.

It looked all smart and pleased with itself. It had had a coat of paint. All the brickwork was painted white, and the woodwork – doors, window frames and so on – were black. There were some designs in black on the white walls, and in white on the black slate roof.

"Those signs must be something danger-ous," thought the hare. He closed his eyes and hopped sideways in the hope that they wouldn't have as much power over him.

As a result he fell into a hole in a flower-bed. Luckily it wasn't too deep.

He looked up and saw a young man with a spade gazing at him.

"Are you okay?" asked the young gar-dener.

The hare, feeling silly, jumped out of the hole. "Fine, fine," he said airily. "Hey! Do you work for the witch?"

"Yes," said the boy, continuing with his digging.

"You shouldn't!" said the hare. "Witches can't be trusted!"

"Is that so?" said the boy. "None of 'em?"

"They're all the same!" answered the hare.

The boy turned his back on the hare and began to whistle while he dug. The hare, who found this annoying, went round to the back of the house and found himself in the kitchen.

There was a beautiful young girl cooking some soup.

"Don't tell me you're working for the witch, too!" said the hare in shocked tones.

"Why not?" asked the girl.

"Well, I mean—! Goodness gracious grips! She's wicked!"

"Oh, do you think so?" asked the girl, tasting the soup.

"What's she told you to put in that soup, for instance?" asked the hare craftily. "Tadpoles and bat's liver, I bet, stuff like that, eh?"

"Oxtail and onions," said the girl. "Same sort of thing."

It seemed useless to go on trying to warn her.

"Is the witch at home?"

"Yes," said the girl. "I was just going to take her some coffee in her spell-room in the cellar."

"You see? You see?" squeaked the hare. "Up to no good! You'd better look out, you'll find yourself turned into a frog, you will!"

"Might be fun to be a frog," said the girl carelessly.

The hare, exasperated, hopped off to find the stairs to the cellar. Soon he was peering round a big oak door with creaking hinges.

The witch was there all right, turning the pages of a huge old book, chewing a pencil and making notes. She was dressed as a witch should be in a long cloak and a pointed hat. But nevertheless the hare gaped at her in astonishment.

Because instead of being a white witch in black-clothes, she was a black witch in white clothes.

"This is too much!" he spluttered. "What kind of magic do you do, anyway? Black magic or white magic?"

"A little of each," said the witch.

"I suppose you'll tell me you do black magic to bad people and white magic to good people!" said the hare.

The witch looked at him, puzzled, her finger keeping her place in the book.

"No, no. The other way round," she said.

Quite baffled by this, the hare sat down and thought. This was not at all what he'd expected.

"Could you do a little spell for me?" he asked at last. "Turn me into something . . . ?"

"I understood you were a magic hare," said the witch.

Uh-oh, not good. She knew about him. He'd have to watch himself.

"Well, yes," he said modestly. "But I can just do the odd trick, vanishing and so on. Beginners' stuff."

"I'm normally only asked to do shape-changes as a punishment. What would you like to be turned into?" asked the witch.

"A person," said the hare at once.

The witch turned round and a smile lit her face. She looked very nice indeed when she smiled, which confused the hare even more.

"Now that is a fun idea," she said. "Let me see. There are plenty of spells in this book for turning people into creatures, but the other way round . . . ! Here's the spell for person-into-hare . . . I've got an idea. Stand still and we'll see if it works."

The hare stood still and the witch read out:

"No more a man who walks upright,
 Be thou a hare and dance all night!
– That's the *right* way round. Now then, let me try it backwards:

'Tine la snad dna rah a outh eb.

Tire-pu skaw ooh nam a rom on.
Goodness, what a tongue-twister!"

She looked up. And up.

Standing before her was a tall young man with a crew-cut, a snub nose and very muscly legs. She took off her glasses and goggled at him, then burst out laughing.

"Great stuff! I did it!" she cried. "And I've even made you good-looking!"

Just then the girl from the kitchen came in with a mug of coffee. She goggled, too. "Who's *that*?" she asked in an admiring voice.

"Like him?" asked the witch smugly. "You can have him." She made a gentle gesture with both hands as if pushing them towards each other.

The hare-lad found himself moving in the direction of the girl, and she came to meet him. She had a breathless, enchanted look. The hare-lad found he had taken her in his arms and kissed her. It felt very, very strange, but he liked it, and was just going to do it again, when she pulled back.

"Wait, though!" said the girl. "I'm in love with the gardener, I don't even know you!" And she gave him a little push and ran out of the room.

"Oh dear," said the witch. "It seems there are some spells even my spells can't compete with." And she chuckled and sipped her coffee.

The hare-lad was feeling some things he'd never felt in all his hare-life. He didn't have names for them (they were things like jealousy and being put down) but he didn't care for any of them.

"I don't like being a person," he said sulkily. "I want to be a hare again."

"What do you say?" asked the witch.

"Please," added the hare crossly.

So the witch said the spell the right way round, and next moment the hare found himself at the right height again, down near the ground. He shook himself and did a short dance to make himself feel all hare again.

The black-and-white witch put down her mug and clapped her hands.

"Great dancing, my friend!" she said. "And now, if you don't mind, I must get on."

"Ah-ha!" cried the hare, remembering what he'd come about. "You have to get on with your wicked spells, isn't that it?"

"The one I'm working on at the moment," said the witch, "is a very hard, new one to close up the hole in the ozone layer. In the sky, you know. It's a tall order, I can tell you, with millions of people working against me. I suppose all those people would agree with you about it being wicked, or they'd be helping me."

The hare hopped slowly and thoughtfully to the door, and then turned.

"And do you call that black magic or white magic?" he asked.

"Definitely black," said the witch with a great big black-and-white grin.

The Hare With the Diamond Tail

There was once a poor king, with nothing in his treasury. He was very keen to find ways to get richer. He taxed his people till they could pay no more. He sold practically everything except his crown. Still the money went out faster than it came in.

He made a proclamation that anyone who could find a way to make him rich could marry his beautiful daughter. (She thought this was a terrible idea, but there wasn't much she could do about it.)

One day, a hunter came to the king. Bowing low before the shabby throne, which hadn't had a coat of gold paint on it for ages, the hunter said:

"Your Majesty, I was out hunting yesterday and I saw a golden hare."

"What do you mean, golden?" asked the king, sitting up.

"I mean it was made of gold, Your Majesty. As the creature dashed across the field, its coat glistened and gleamed. It was pure gold, I promise you. If I can catch that hare, may I marry the princess?"

"Well," said the king cautiously, "you catch it first and then we'll see. But I give it a qualified 'yes'."

Before the first hunter was out of the palace, a second one had arrived.

"Your Majesty!" he cried. "Did you know there is a hare running about your kingdom that has ruby eyes?"

"Ruby eyes!" exclaimed the king. "Are you sure about this?"

"I saw it myself. I was hunting through a thicket and I saw these two red rubies shining out of a bush. They must be worth a fortune, they are so huge."

"Catch me that hare," said the king excitedly, rubbing his hands with glee, "and the princess is yours!" He forgot he'd half promised her to the first fellow, and began thinking about all he could do with the price of two big rubies.

But half an hour later, a third hunter arrived, quite breathless.

"Your Majesty! I have seen a hare with a diamond tail!"

"WHAAAT!" cried the king, jumping up and down.

"Yes," said the hunter. "I was hunting at night, and I saw it, a giant white diamond flickering through the wood as the hare ran!"

"A hare with a diamond tail!" said the king, practically drooling with eagerness. "If you can catch that hare, I'll give you my daughter's hand, and my second-best palace to live in!" He'd forgotten all about the other two, and shook hands on his new bargain.

The three hunters were now combing the countryside in search of the fabulous hares they had seen. Day and night they hunted, but they saw nothing unusual.

And the princess breathed again, for she had seen all three of the hunters from her bedroom window and she thought they were totally unfanciable. She fancied her father's gamekeeper's son, who was eighteen and had a mop of curly hair and kind hands.

The king was a great gossip, so very soon the kingdom was abuzz with tales of the golden hare, and the one with ruby eyes, and the one with a diamond tail that were going to make the king rich.

The princess spoke to her friend the gamekeeper's son.

"Do you think there could be such creatures?"

"Naaaa," said the lad. "Shouldn't think so for a minute."

"If there were, and you could catch one, you could marry me," she mentioned modestly.

The lad, who'd never dared to do more than dream, saw he was in with a chance.

"Right, I'll keep an eye out," he said.

The next day at noon when he was feeding his (or rather, the king's) pheasants, he suddenly saw something flash across the field. It was a hare, and its coat shone like something on fire. But the boy knew it was only a trick of the sunlight.

That evening, when he was shutting the pheasants up, he heard a little rustle in the bushes. He looked up and saw two bright red eyes looking at him. But he knew they were only catching the glow of the sunset.

That night, as he was walking through the woods to check that there were no poachers, he saw a hare dashing ahead of him through the trees. It snowy tail reflected the light of his torch and looked just like a big diamond.

Suddenly the boy let out a roar of laughter.

"Those great fools!" he sputtered. "Call theirselves hunters!" And he sat down very quietly in the darkened wood to wait.

After a while the hare approached him. He sat so still it didn't see him, and as it bounded past, he reached out, quick as thought, and caught it by the ears.

"You be comin' with me to the palace, young fellow," he said.

He carried it straight to the king.

"Here be your golden hare," he said, "*and* your ruby-eyed hare, AND your diamond-tailed hare, all in one. And now can I marry your daughter?"

The king was blazing mad. "You stupid lout!" he screamed. "That's a perfectly ordinary hare! How dare you come in here with your dirty boots asking for my daughter's hand!"

But the lad stood his ground. He explained to the king how the hunters had made their mistakes. The king was so disappointed he burst into tears.

"You mean I won't be rich after all?" he blubbed.

But at that moment, the hare leapt out of the lad's hands, and began to perform a wonderful dance in front of the king. He danced on his hind legs, he turned somersaults, he did huge leaps – and the amazing thing was, that as he danced, he *sang*. He sang a ballad, which is a song that tells a story.

He sang about three foolish hunters and a sensible gamekeeper's son, and how kings could be good kings and go down in history even if they weren't rich, and he sang about true love which knows no rank and has no care for wealth.

The king and all the court were entranced. And the king very humbly asked the hare if he would perform in public, for money, and the hare agreed, provided the lad could marry the princess. The king was so impressed with the words of the song that he stopped

overtaxing his people, and even gave the lad a clean pair of boots to be married in.

I won't add that the lad and the princess lived happily ever after, because they had rows from time to time, like anyone else, especially when the lad forgot to wipe his boots. But then she would remind herself that she had nearly had to marry one of those boring, stupid hunters, and she would forgive him.

The Hare and the
Wicked Uncle

Robin and Rupert lived with their uncle. Why, they were not sure. And he would never tell them.

Once, Rupert, who was the elder, plucked up courage to ask him.

"Haven't we got any mum and dad?"

His uncle, who was busy, didn't answer. So Rupert asked him again. This time his uncle turned round sharply and said, "Maybe you have and maybe you haven't. Now push off."

No prizes for guessing whether Robin and Rupert liked their uncle a lot or enjoyed living with him. He behaved as if everything he had to do just to keep the boys alive was a trouble and a burden.

But the worst thing was the way he behaved about Robin's illness.

Robin was quite ill. He had been for a long time. It was a funny sort of illness. He didn't have to stay in bed all the time. There were times when he felt all right. Then he would go to school. But he had to visit a doctor regularly. Sometimes the doctor looked pleased, but usually he didn't look anything. Robin took this for a bad sign, and said to Rupert:

"I think I'm getting worse. What do you think?"

Rupert always said, "You don't look any worse to me. If you ask me, you're getting better." This often cheered Robin up for the moment.

But their uncle didn't cheer him up.

"Illness is a judgement," he growled, more than once. "Illness happens because of wrong-doing. It's a punishment."

Robin never dared ask what he'd done to deserve his illness, but Rupert did. Just once.

"But what's Robin done, Uncle? He hasn't done anything!"

His uncle turned on him, red in the face.

"Who are you to decide? Don't you dare contradict me! If he hadn't done wrong, he wouldn't be ill. Not another word out of you!"

The boys' favourite thing to do was to go exploring in the countryside near their uncle's home (well, it was their home too, but they usually thought of it as "Uncle's house".) It was a bit of a way, and lately Rupert had had to give Robin some serious help to walk the last part.

As soon as they were clear of the town, Robin always felt better. He couldn't really run properly any more, but Rupert stuck with him and they followed their favourite paths through the woods and climbed the style into their favourite field.

It happened to be the hare's field.

The hare had often seen them there. He'd watched them running and playing; then just playing; nowadays, walking rather slowly, and sitting down a lot.

They had a special place near an old hollow tree that they liked. Robin had lots of stories in his head about that tree and the magic creatures who lived in it. Rupert made him tell them, old ones and new ones (when Robin could think them up) over and over again. And the hare crept close, though keeping hidden, to listen. He loved stories.

One day he was amazed to hear Robin telling a story about *him*!

"I had a dream about a magic hare," he began. "He lives in this field and this is his best tree. He likes it because it's got the hole in it. That's where he goes to think up magic tricks to play on the other animals."

"I beg your pardon!" the hare interrupted before he could stop himself. "Me, play tricks on other animals? No such thing! Not my style at all!"

The boys had spun round and were gaping at him.

"It can't have been me you dreamt about," went on the hare firmly.

"But – but it was!" gasped Robin. "It was just like you – exactly! And you did do tricks! Like, you bunged up a dog's mouth to stop it barking."

"I did not! Dogs are meant to bark."

"And you stuck a pig's legs together so that it rolled over and over."

"That's an absolute lie! Ask anyone!"

"*And* you waited till an owl's head was twisted round backwards and then you fixed it like that so it couldn't see where it was flying."

"I have *never* in my *life* – oh. Wait a bit. Yes, I might have done, when it had its eye on a fieldmouse. But as soon as the mouse ran off, I untwisted the owl straight away. It could have hurt itself. But not the other things, I swear!"

"A dream's only a dream," Rupert said. "They're all mixed up. Still, it's funny you dreamt a magic hare, and now here he is."

There was a silence. Both the boys were thinking.

"Can you do any magic you like?" asked Rupert cautiously.

"I know what you're going to ask," said the hare soberly. "I'm sorry. I'd do it if I could. I can only do small things really."

The boys knew that to make Robin well would be a very big thing, too big for a little magic hare.

The hare felt very sad. "Is there any small thing I could do?" he asked. "I mean, would a little dance cheer you up?"

"Oh, yes!" exclaimed both the boys.

So the hare danced for them. And as they watched his antics, entranced, Robin found himself feeling better every minute. He was ready to jump up and join in, when suddenly there was an almighty BANG.

The hare instantly vanished.

The boys got a terrible fright. The bang had come from the other side of the tree. Rupert edged his head round, and saw his uncle with a shotgun.

When he saw the boys, he let out a roar.

"You young idiots! I might have shot you!" he shouted. "You never think of me, do you? I would have gone to jail!" He came stamping towards them in a blazing temper. "Where's that animal?"

He was searching in the grass. The boys cowered at the foot of the tree.

"I *know* I hit him! Come on, what did you do with him? Hide him in the hollow tree? You'll be sorry! Let me look!"

Rupert jumped aside. Robin, who felt completely weak again since the hare had disappeared, didn't move.

"Get out of my way, you wretched little cripple!" shouted the uncle.

He reached out as if to thrust Robin away. But abruptly he stopped, and his face, which had been bright red, turned pea green, and then a terrified, frozen white.

The boys looked at the tree, where their uncle was staring.

Out of the hole in its trunk came a furry face, followed by long ears, followed by a hare's body. But it was like blowing a bubble. As the hare emerged, he swelled and grew bigger and bigger. And bigger. And BIGGER.

The uncle reeled back. He tried to raise his shotgun but it dropped from his trembling hands. He fell over backwards in the grass as the vast, enormous, giant hare loomed before him, half as tall as the tree trunk and twice as wide.

The hare silently opened its huge mouth.

The boys gasped. They thought he was about to eat their uncle! But instead the hare very calmly picked him up in its teeth, turned round, popped him into the hole in the tree (which had mysteriously become just large enough), did the same with the gun, and suddenly – poof!

The hare was his right size again. A little furry animal, looking rather tired. And the tree hadn't got a hole any more. The hole had closed right up.

Rupert and Robin were stunned. They hadn't been frightened of the hare, even when he was a giant one, but they felt rather uncomfortable now.

"Who shall we live with?" asked Rupert.

"Boys belong with their parents," said the hare. "So I'd always heard."

"Our parents? You mean – we have some?"

The hare had closed his eyes as if thinking deeply.

"They're rather a long way off," he said. "And they're not together. They both seem to be pretty unhappy . . . Perhaps I could put some thoughts into their heads . . . Quite a big job, that. It'll take time."

The boys didn't say anything. They both felt the matter was urgent.

"And while I'm working on it," said the hare briskly, "I think you'd better live with me. I'll look after you."

The next moment, both the boys felt their bodies shrinking. It was the weirdest feeling! As they shrank towards the ground, they felt themselves changing.

They fell on to all fours. Their ears were growing. Their legs felt as if they needed to jump. All kinds of strong smells came into their noses. They found they were covered with fur! They stared at each other out of round, glassy eyes.

"Robin! You're a hare!"

"So are you!"

"Well, I can't look after a pair of *boys* in my burrow," said the hare reasonably. "Don't worry, it's great fun being a hare. And of course, hares can't have a human illness, so . . ."

Robin took off. He simply took off. He bounded and leapt, he jumped and capered. He felt magnificent!

"I love being a hare!" he shouted. "Can I stay one for ever?"

"There are limits to being a hare," said the hare. "But while you are one, go ahead, enjoy yourself!"

And the two boy-hares raced and romped and chased each other through the grass, while inside the tree the wicked uncle raged and roared and raved and battered, to no avail.

And far away, two sad lonely people who had given up their children when they parted, each received a sudden, compelling thought, and began making plans to find their boys and each other.

The Hare and his Magic

The hare thought he should be popular with all the other animals. He did tricks for them, he danced and sang to entertain them, he helped them with all kinds of special favours when they were in trouble. He thought he was a very nice fellow.

But sometimes it seemed as if the others resented him.

"Why are you able to do magic, when we can't?" grumbled the cow one day.

"You can do magic," said the hare promptly.

"Me? No I can't," said the cow.

"Of course you can! You don't think turning grass into milk, cheese and butter is magic?"

"Oh, *that*," said the cow. "Any fool can do that."

"Well, I can't," said the hare, "and nor can a pig or a horse or a hen or—"

"Who are you calling a hen?" said the hen. "Telling me what I can't do! Who wants to make cheese anyway?" She pecked at a seed and ate it thoughtfully. "Tell me what I *can* do, if you're so clever. And *don't* say 'lay eggs', because that's not magic."

"It is to me," said the hare. "And to the cow, and to lots of other creatures. We can't do that."

"Oh yes? I bet you could make an egg out of thin air if you wanted to. I saw you open a hole in a field with a wave of your paw the other day, to let the fox in when the hounds were after him."

"The fox could have done that for himself if he'd just had more time," said the hare, trying to look modest. "He's a terrific digger. I just speeded things up a little, that's all."

The sheepdog had moseyed over to listen.

"What magic can I do?" he asked eagerly.

"You can do one of the greatest tricks of all," said the hare promptly. "You can understand human speech and obey it."

"I can do that a bit, too," said the horse, sticking her head over a hedge. "Does that mean I'm a magic animal like you?"

"Ah. Well, not quite like me perhaps," said the hare, his conceit getting the better of him. He wanted the others to feel better, but he was not about to let them think they were as brilliant as he was.

"That's it! There he goes!" snorted the pig from the next field. "Bragging about his talents! Well, I'm not magic and I don't want to be. I'm just a plain, honest-to-goodness farmyard animal. I eat just about anything I'm given and I get fat on it. Given half a chance, I can turn a patch of ground from a useless, weed-choked wilderness into a rich, clean, well-dug patch just waiting to be turned into a garden. Of course, I can't do it with a wave of my trotter. It takes time and effort. All the greatest achievements do."

The other animals, reminded that laying eggs and making milk and being ridden and obeying orders all take time and effort, all agreed loudly.

"Yeah, that's right!"

"That's telling him!"

"Takes effort!"

"Takes time!"

"All the greatest achievements!"

"And if it doesn't – it isn't! That's for sure!"

The hare hopped away. He felt awful. What! His magic was worthless because he could do it so easily?

He sat in a private part of the wood and did a few tricks to console himself.

He hexed an acorn so that it grew into an oak in five minutes, but in growing so fast it made three other ordinary trees fall down.

He conjured a passing beetle into a small dinosaur, but it looked so out of place and lonely that he hastily changed it back.

He thought he'd do something small, natural and useful. He put some magic on a drop of rainwater and turned it into a very pretty fountain.

Several small animals approached it for a drink and the hare thought he'd made a real achievement – until a falcon, attracted by the sound and sparkle of the water, came swooping down and carried off a fieldmouse in one foot and a vole in the other. Shocked, the hare hurriedly shrank the fountain down to a raindrop again, and wandered off gloomily.

"All the talents the others have are useful and harmless," he thought. "My magic is terrible. It's a nuisance. It's dangerous, sometimes. And it makes all the others jealous of me." He wondered if he could magic his magic away altogether, and just be ordinary like his fellow animals.

But could he bear to be just ordinary? Not be able to do magic tricks whenever he felt like it? He was so used to being a magic animal.

He came to the middle of a field and began one of his spring dances. There was no audience to applaud him. He just felt like it.

He did a few leaps at first, and then, gradually getting into the spirit of the thing, he began turning and whirling in the air, doing backovers and frontovers, flinging his legs in all directions. He felt the wind in his fur and the ground like great springs under his dancing feet. Higher and higher he leapt, no longer showing off, just doing it for himself.

He had never enjoyed a dance so much. But he didn't realise that a little magic had crept in – it was his nature, after all. With a last great leap, he soared up through the atmosphere, through the stratosphere, through dark and empty space, and landed on the moon.

He couldn't breathe! (That's because there's no air on the moon.)

In the nick of time before he choked, he magicked a small hare-shaped spacesuit for himself.

There! That was better. He began to hop about, exploring. It was very bare here – no grass, no trees, no streams. He decided to make some.

"Nobody likes me down there," he thought. "Right. I'll stay up here and make my own magic world." And he waved his paw.

Nothing happened. The moon stayed cold, grey and empty.

What was this? Then he understood. His spacesuit blocked off his magic powers. Up here, it was a question of dying for lack of air, or not being able to do any magic.

He looked back down to earth. It was beautiful, all blue and swirly white. Down there somewhere was everything he was used to. And all his mates . . . Not that he

missed that ungrateful bunch, oh no! Not that he was ever going to do any magic for *them* again. Not if they begged him – not if they were in the worst scrapes imaginable!

But still ... he couldn't very well live up here, all dark and cold and with nothing growing and nothing to eat or drink ... There wasn't much choice, really. He shut his eyes, brought all his magic to bear, and dived off the moon into space.

When he got back he breathed a deep sigh of happiness, and buried the spacesuit in an old badger sett. He could have magicked it away but he'd decided not to use magic any more. No way! Never! Not if they begged in chorus! He would just be an ordinary animal.

But no sooner had he definitely and positively made up his mind to this, than he heard a shout.

"Hare! Hare! Come quick!"

Someone in trouble!

Hare bolted through the grass as fast as he could, mustering up his magic powers as he went.